Dragons and Dinosaurs

by Janet Perry and Victor Gentle

For Craig Gustafson and Rich Douglas, each of whom cheerily vanquishes dragons on a daily basis with a deft flick of his wit

Gareth Stevens Publishing

MILWAUKEE

For a free color catalog describing Gareth Stevens' list of high-quality books and multimedia programs, call 1-800-542-2595 (USA) or 1-800-461-9120 (Canada). Gareth Stevens Publishing's Fax: (414) 225-0377.

Library of Congress Cataloging-in-Publication Data

Perry, Janet, 1960-
   Dragons and dinosaurs / by Janet Perry and Victor Gentle.
      p. cm. — (Monsters: an imagination library series)
   Includes bibliographical references (p. 22) and index.
   Summary: Discusses dragons as they have appeared in the beliefs and legends of various cultures, including ancient Babylon and Egypt, Europe, and Asia, as well as how they are reflected in real creatures such as dinosaurs and komodo lizards.
   ISBN 0-8368-2436-9 (lib. bdg.)
   1. Dragons—Juvenile literature. 2. Dinosaurs—Juvenile literature. [1. Dragons. 2. Folklore.] I. Gentle, Victor. II. Title. III. Series: Perry, Janet, 1960- Monsters.
GR830.D7P47   1999
398.24'54—dc21
                                          99-25566

398.24 P   9690720

Dragons and dinosaurs /

First published in 1999 by
Gareth Stevens Publishing
1555 North RiverCenter Drive, Suite 201
Milwaukee, WI 53212 USA

Text: Janet Perry and Victor Gentle
Page layout: Janet Perry, Victor Gentle, and Helene Feider
Cover design: Joel Bucaro and Helene Feider
Series editor: Patricia Lantier-Sampon
Editorial assistant: Diane Laska

Images from the Art Institute of Chicago: p. 7: Bernardo Martorell, Spanish (Catalonian), c. 1400-1452, Saint George Killing the Dragon, tempera on panel, 1430-35, 155.3 x 98 cm, Gift of Mrs. Richard E. Danielson and Mrs. Chauncey McCormick, 1933.786

p. 13: Katsukawa Shunshô, Japanese, 1726-1792, The Actors Sawamura Sojuro II as the Chinese Sage Kosekiko on Horseback, and Ichikawa Danzo III as the Chinese Warrior Choryo Seated on a Dragon, woodblock print, 1768, 14.9 x 32.5 cm, Clarence Buckingham Collection, 1925.2411

Editor's note: Choryo is the Japanese name for the Chinese warrior Zhang Liang.

Photo credits: Cover, pp. 15, 17, 19 © Photofest; p. 5 © Dembinsky Photo Associates/Stan Osolinski; pp. 7, 13 Photograph © 1998 The Art Institute of Chicago; p. 9 Illustration by Gustaf Tenggren from A WONDER-BOOK AND TANGLEWOOD TALES by Nathaniel Hawthorne. Illustrations copyright 1923, and (c) renewed 1951 by Houghton Mifflin Company. Reprinted by permission of Houghton Mifflin Company. All rights reserved.; p. 11 Illustration by Arthur Rackham from *The Ring of the Nibelung,* 1911; p. 21 © Gerald Cubitt/Picture Perfect

Printed in the United States of America

1 2 3 4 5 6 7 8 9 03 02 01 00 99

TABLE OF CONTENTS

Words that appear in the glossary are printed in **boldface**
type the first time they occur in the text.

DRAGON SNACK

You crash your plane in a remote jungle. Your instruments have been haywire for the last six hours, and you've been flying through thick clouds. You have no idea where you are. You survived the landing. It's a miracle.

You stumble from your plane — *spah-latt!* — right into the muck. As you unsquish your eyes, you gaze into the snaky, staring peepers of a BIG lizard. You feel like a snack . . . *its* snack.

Its mouth is scaly, and its breath stinks.

It introduces itself, *"RrrowwrrRRR!"*

"Yikes!" you whisper. "A **dragon**!"

4

Marine iguanas look ferocious but, in fact, they only eat seaweed. However, they get rid of extra salt from their food with a mighty spit, so stand back!

DEMON DRAGONS

Was that lizard a dragon? Maybe so, maybe not. Maybe it depends on what you mean by dragon . . . .

Many cultures say that the world began as a humongous, topsy-turvy mess, a playground for monsters and dragons. Gods and heroes brought order and civilization to the world by imprisoning some dragons and killing the rest.

Yet, no matter how well-ordered the world became, disease, disorder, disaster, or destruction would strike. When evil fell upon the Earth, people thought dragons were on the loose.

St. George saves a North African king's daughter from a dragon that is about to devour her. This story represents the triumph of Christianity over evil.

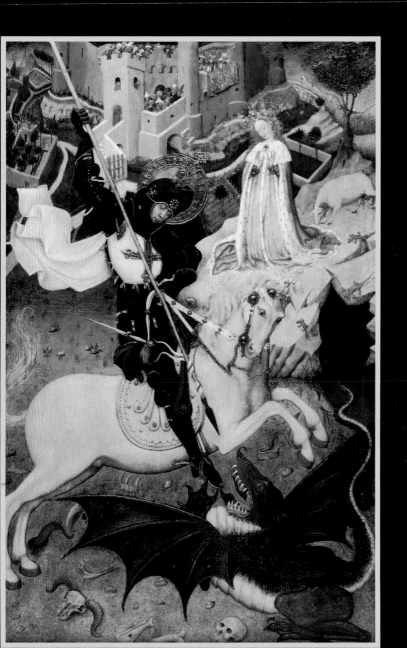

DRAGON DEFEATS

Ancient **Babylonians** believed that the enemy of order was Tiamat, a dragon. She was the mother of their most powerful god, Marduk. By splitting Tiamat in half, Marduk created heaven and Earth.

Ancient Egyptians believed that the sun-god Ra had to battle a dragon named Apep every night just to bring light to the world each new day.

Ancient **Norse** peoples believed that a giant tree named Yggdrasil held all creation together. Nidhoggr, a dragon that lived under the world, chewed at the roots of the tree. He was trying to ruin everything, of course!

The Greek hero Cadmus slays the dragon that killed his comrades. Soldiers spring from the dragon's teeth and help Cadmus build the city of Thebes.

DRAGONS TO THE WEST . . .

In European stories, dragons lived in mountains, oceans, lakes, rivers, or swamps. They had wings, claws, fangs, horns, one or more heads, or eyes made of jewels. Their bodies might be part serpent, part bird, part lion, and part lizard.

Although dragons came in many forms and lived in many places, European heroes always knew dragons when they saw them.

Dragons breathed fire and sickness. Their spit dissolved rock and metal. They wore scales that were stronger than the best armor. Oh, and they were BIG!

In the German **legend** *The Ring of the Nibelung*, the gnome Alberrich magically becomes a dragon. Here, Loge tricks him into becoming a toad and steals his treasure.

... AND DRAGONS TO THE EAST!

In Asian stories, dragons are part of the order in the world — but they are as unpredictable as the weather.

When the Indian god Vishnu, the Lord of the Universe, took a breather from work, he slept on the back of a dragon that had eleven heads.

Chinese dragons protected treasures, such as gold and jade, underground. They ruled the water, protected riverbanks, and made the water flow. They protected the sky and made weather.

The ancient Chinese warrior Zhang Liang rides a river dragon to return a wise man's shoe in a test of Zhang's character. He passed the test!

LET SLEEPING DRAGONS LIE

In Japanese stories, dragons get vicious when they are rudely disturbed.

The original *Godzilla, King of the Monsters* is a 1956 Japanese movie. In the movie, Godzilla, a huge beast, rises out of the sea after a **nuclear bomb** attack on Japan. This skyscraper-sized lizard breathes **radioactive** fire, causes earthquakes and hurricanes, and smashes the city of Tokyo.

Before he was poisoned with **nuclear waste**, Godzilla was much smaller. Even so, he kept the natives of a small island near Japan in fear. The islanders would buy their safety each year by sacrificing a maiden to him.

Godzilla takes a brisk jog along a New York street in the 1998 Hollywood remake of the 1956 Japanese movie classic.

TOKOYO SAVES THE DAY

Godzilla is an ancient dragon, according to the islanders. Islanders have seen his kind before . . . .

In an old Japanese tale, an emperor has a fit of temper and **banishes** one of his bravest warriors to a dragon's island.

The warrior's daughter, Tokoyo, searches for her beloved father and finds her way to the dragon's island. There, she finds a poor family's only daughter about to be sacrificed to protect against storms caused by the dragon. She chooses to take the girl's place.

Valiantly, Tokoyo kills the dragon. Both her father and the girl are saved!

Japanese legends of sea dragons have inspired many modern monster movies. Here, a dragon-like **dinosaur** rises from the deep for a snack.

ARE DRAGONS OF OLD JUST ANCIENT FOSSILS?

Why do so many people tell stories about dragons? Why did people believe dragons were real? Did they, perhaps, have good reasons?

Let's say you do not know about dinosaurs, but you have heard about dragons. One day, you find a huge **fossil**, a giant lizard's head, with lots and lots of teeth. You might just decide that this is the skull of a dragon.

In fact, some lizards that are alive today have "dragon" in their name. *Draco volens*, the "flying dragon," catches insects as it glides through the wetlands of southern Asia on wings made of skin.

A model *T. rex* from the movie *Jurassic Park* (1993) flashes its fangs. Add wings and a fiery belch, and it could easily pass for a dragon.

THERE'S REASON TO BELIEVE

You may not believe in powerful dragons or whether they cause destruction or keep order.

However, unknown *things* do creep over Earth. Just to prove it, a komodo dragon surprised a pilot who crash-landed on a remote Indonesian island in 1912. It was rather small for a komodo, only 5 feet (1.5 meters) long and weighing 125 pounds (57 kilograms). Although this "dragon" was new to modern science, komodos had been around for thousands of years.

So, if you fall into the muck on a remote island, don't be too surprised — when you unsquish your eyes, you may see a real, live dragon.

Komodo dragons are ferocious monitor lizards that grow to 10 feet (3 m) long, weigh up to 300 pounds (136 kg), have stinky breath, and devour pigs, deer, and water buffalos!

MORE TO READ, VIEW, AND LISTEN TO

Books (Nonfiction)

America's Very Own Monsters. Daniel Cohen (Dodd, Mead)

Dawn to Dusk in the Galápagos: Flightless Birds, Swimming Lizards, and Other Fascinating Creatures. Rita Golden Gelman (Little, Brown)

Komodo! Peter Sis (Greenwillow Books)

The Living World. Record Breakers (series). David Lambert (Gareth Stevens)

Monsters (series). Janet Perry and Victor Gentle (Gareth Stevens)

The New Dinosaur Collection (series). (Gareth Stevens)

Real Live Monsters! Ellen Schecter (Gareth Stevens)

Snakes, Salamanders, and Lizards. Young Naturalist Field Guides (series). Diane L. Burns (Gareth Stevens)

World of Dinosaurs (series). (Gareth Stevens)

Books (Activity)

Chinese Cultural Activities. (ARTS, Inc.)

Dragons and Prehistoric Monsters. Draw, Model, and Paint (series). Isidro Sánchez (Gareth Stevens)

Monster Jokes. Diane Dow Suire (Children's Press)

Books (Fiction)

The Complete Book of Dragons. E. Nesbit (Macmillan)

Delicious Hullabaloo: Pachanga Deliciosa. Pat Mora (Piñata Books)

Godzilla: Journey to Monster Island. Scott Ciencin (Random House)

The Golem and the Dragon Girl. Sonia Levitin (Dial Books)

The Knight and the Dragon. Tomie de Paola (Putnam)

Norby and the Oldest Dragon. Janet Asimov and Isaac Asimov (Walker & Co.)

Sim Chung and the River Dragon. Ellen Schecter (Gareth Stevens)

Videos (Nonfiction)

Monster. (DK Vision: BBC Worldwide Americas)

Videos (Fiction)

Dinosaur! Giant Birds of the Air: The Tale of a Feather. (A&E)

The Giant Behemoth. (Warner Studios)

Giant Gila Monsters. (Victory Audio Video)

Godzilla, King of the Monsters. (Toho)

WEB SITES

If you have your own computer and Internet access, great! If not, most libraries have Internet access. Go to your library and enter the word *museums* into the library's preferred search engine. See if you can find a museum web page that has exhibits on fossils, lizards, amphibians, snakes, Oriental history, and art. If any of these museums are close by, you can visit them in person!

The Internet changes every day, and web sites come and go. We believe the sites we recommend here are likely to last, and give the best and most appropriate links for our readers to pursue their interest in the folklore of dragons, the history and science of dinosaurs, and many related subjects.

www.ajkids.com

This is the junior *Ask Jeeves* site – a great research tool.

Some questions to *Ask Jeeves Kids*:
- *What lizard is the biggest in the world?*
- *Are there lizards that live in Iceland?*
- *What was the largest dinosaur?*
- *Is there a sport that has* dragon *in its name?*

You can also type in words and phrases with a "?" at the end, for example,
- *Chinese dragons?*
- *Gilas?*
- *Godzilla?*
- *St. George and the Dragon?*

www.mzoo.com

The Miniature Zoo has a special section of monsters and weird critters. Go to the site and click on the Quick Site Index to see pictures and links to many strange and unusual beasties in myth, legend, and history, including modern-day "dragons"!

www.yahooligans.com

This is the junior Yahoo! home page. Click on one of the listed topics (such as Around the World, Science and Nature) for more links. From Around the World, try Anthropology and Archaeology and Mythology and Folklore to find more sites on dragons. From Science and Nature, you might try Dinosaurs, Animals, Living Things, or Museums and Exhibits to find out more about lizards, dinosaurs, and other dragonlike animals. You can also search for more information by typing a word in the Yahooligans search engine. Some words to try are: *dragon, flying dragon, Galápagos Islands, gila monster, komodo dragon.*

GLOSSARY

You can find these words on the pages listed. Reading a word in a sentence helps you understand it even better.

Babylonian — of ancient Babylonia, a country that existed in the Middle East from about 4,000 to about 2,500 years ago 8

banishes — sends away, as a punishment 16

dinosaurs (DIE-noh-sarz) — giant reptiles that lived on Earth millions of years ago 16, 18

dragons — imaginary creatures that are usually thought of as large, lizardlike, or snakelike monsters that breathe fire and have wings 4, 6, 8, 10, 12, 14, 16, 18, 20

fossils — the remains of plants or animals from hundreds, thousands, or millions of years ago found embedded in rock 18

legend — a story from earlier times 10

Norse — of or from ancient Scandinavia, which consisted of the modern-day countries of Denmark, Norway, Sweden, and, possibly, Finland and Iceland, or of the peoples who lived there 8

nuclear bombs (NU-klee-er BOMZ) — very destructive bombs that release huge amounts of energy stored inside atoms 14

nuclear waste — the dangerous radioactive remains after a nuclear bomb explodes, or the radioactive leftovers from an atomic power station 14

radioactive — giving off rays as a result of the natural decay and artificial splitting of some atoms 14

INDEX